This Topsy and Tim book belongs to

_____

Topsy and Tim Go to the Dentist

By Jean and Gareth Adamson

Dental Advisors: the British Dental Health Foundation

Illustrations by Belinda Worsley

A catalogue record for this book is available from the British Library

This title was previously published as part of the Topsy and Tim Learnabout series
Published by Ladybird Books Ltd
A Penguin Company
Penguin Books Ltd., 80 Strand, London WC2R 0RL, UK
Penguin Books Australia Ltd., Camberwell, Victoria, Australia
Penguin Group (NZ) 67 Apollo Drive, Rosedale, North Shore 0632, New Zealand

003 –
3 5 7 9 10 8 6 4

ISBN: 978-1-40930-058-8
Printed in China

www.topsyandtim.com

It was time for Topsy and Tim to visit the dentist. Mummy took them to see Mrs Berry, the dentist at the Health Centre. They sat in the waiting room and read comics.

The dentist's door opened and out came Josie Miller and her mummy. Josie smiled at Topsy and Tim.

"I've got to wear a brace on my teeth," she said.
"Why?" asked Topsy.
"To make my teeth straight," said Josie.
"Mrs Berry is ready to see you now, Topsy and Tim," said the nurse.

"Hello twins," said Mrs Berry.

"Your surgery smells funny!" said Topsy.

"It's a nice clean smell," said Mummy.

"Who wants to go first?" said Mrs Berry.

"ME!" said Tim.

He climbed into the dentist's chair. Mrs Berry pressed a button and the chair tilted back. Tim felt like a rocket pilot. Mrs Berry put a disposable mask over her nose and mouth.

"What's that for?" asked Tim.

"So that I don't breathe over you," said Mrs Berry.

"Open wide and let me see your teeth," said Mrs Berry. Tim opened his mouth as wide as he could.

"This small mirror will help me look for holes in Tim's teeth," said Mrs Berry. "Little holes can turn into big holes and big holes can turn into toothache!"
There were no little holes in Tim's teeth.

"Your turn now, Topsy," said Mrs Berry.
She found a little hole in one of Topsy's teeth.
"I'll clean that hole and put a filling in it," said Mrs Berry.
"It will stop pieces of food getting in and turning nasty."
First, Mrs Berry hung a sucking tube in Topsy's mouth.
"That's to stop you dribbling,"
she said.

The tube made funny sucking noises. Then she used her whizzy drill to clean out the hole in Topsy's tooth.

The nurse gave Topsy a glass of pink water to rinse her mouth. Then Mrs Berry dried the hole with a little air blower, so that the filling would stick tight inside it.

The nurse mixed a tiny bit of silver filling. Tim watched her. "That's Topsy's filling," she said.

Mrs Berry pushed the silver
filling into the hole in Topsy's
tooth. She pressed it down
and made it perfectly smooth.

"There! Good as new!" said Mrs Berry.

"Did it hurt?" asked Tim.

"The drill was noisy," said Topsy. "But it didn't hurt."

"You've both got good teeth," said Mrs Berry. "Keep them that way. Eat lots of different foods but remember, sweet foods can hurt your teeth, so don't eat them too often."

"Never forget to clean your teeth in the morning and at bedtime with a fluoride toothpaste, and don't eat or drink in bed."

"Not even water?" said Tim.

"Only water," said Mrs Berry. "Sweet drinks can hurt your teeth as much as sweet food."

Mrs Berry gave Topsy and Tim a badge each to remind them to look after their teeth.

"Come back and see me soon," she said.

Before they went home
the receptionist wrote down
the date of their next visit.
A little boy came into the waiting room with his mummy.

He was trying not to cry.
"It's Tony Welch," said Topsy.
"What's the matter, Tony?" asked Tim.
"I've got toothache," sniffed Tony.
"He eats too many sweets," said Tony's mum.
"Never mind," said Topsy. "Mrs Berry
will make it better."

On the way home they passed a sweet shop.
"I would like some sweets," said Topsy, "but I don't want
toothache like Tony."
"There are other nice things that are better for you," said Mummy.

She bought them lovely crunchy apples from the greengrocer.

Then they went to the chemist's to buy new toothbrushes. The chemist told them about disclosing tablets.

"Just chew half a tablet, then rinse your mouth with water," he explained. "The parts of your teeth that most need cleaning will turn pink."

"We'd look funny going to school with pink teeth," said Tim.

The chemist laughed.
"You clean away the pink bits with your new toothbrushes," he said.
"When there is no pink left, you know your teeth are clean."

As soon as they got home, Topsy and Tim tried out their new toothbrushes.

"Mrs Berry won't find any holes in our teeth next visit," said Topsy and Tim.

*Now turn the page and help
Topsy and Tim solve a puzzle.*

Do you know which things are good for
your teeth and which things are bad?
Follow the lines to find out what Topsy
and Tim and their friends have chosen.

A Map of the Village

farm

Topsy and
Tim's house

Tony's
house

Kerr'
hou

park

garage

health
centre

post
office

church

primary school

nursery school

police station

Look out for other titles in the series.

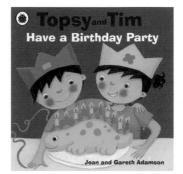

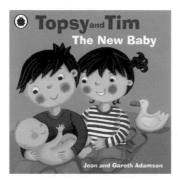

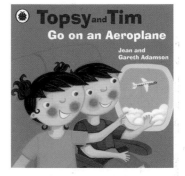

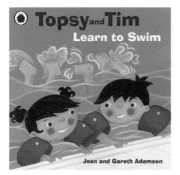

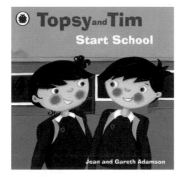

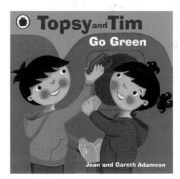

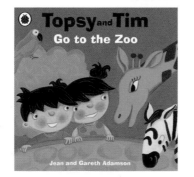

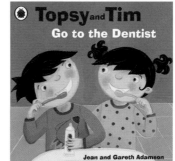